WAR IN THE TIME OF LOVE

LEN QUIMBY

Primal Publishing · Allston, Massachusetts

Book design by Michael McInnis
Cover illustration used with permission.

ISBN 978-1-971785-00-4

Primal Publishing
POBox 1179
Allston, MA 02134

No one claims credit for the worst of the terror.
—Don DeLillo, *The Names.*

WAR IN THE TIME OF LOVE

THE 21ST CENTURY AND HOW TO LEAVE IT

This is how they left the 21st Century:

A nimbus of ash that chewed its way through their lives, etching our screens. Had the television finally blinkered out, exhausted its usefulness when we needed it most. The cloud reminded us of late night television snow, before 24-hour broadcasting, before time and memory existed on taped archives. Finally, television had attained a clarity we had not seen before. It was the city, the country, the world that had signed off the air.

This is how they left the 21st Century:

In the dark a single light clamped to a transom where artists, writers, musicians found, at long last, a connection to the rest of world and sat in metal folding chairs in the long, narrow hallway of a dingy building, raising money for the victims of an attack.

In that hallway, among his friends and lovers and ex-lovers and those who had long lost the ability of love, Sonny sat with the ghosts of all who died, of all who had died in the neighborhood, in the only city in America named after an artist.

It is not the dying that Sonny fears, or even the method of his death, a suicide. He does not fear the infamy that will attach to his name. In the darkest recesses of his mind, a place he only goes when he is using crystal meth, his biggest fear is the void. As if he were an astronaut adrift, endless, weightless, but always returning, cartwheeling through the cosmos, frozen.

There is an itch beneath the straps of the back pack straining with the weight of its terrible truth. He can feel the itch spread out, spiking across his stomach and up to his neck.

Sonny exhales and pushes the button gripped in his sweating hand.

The explosion blows apart the top floor of the building, splintering it and them onto the street, a moiety radiating across the neighborhood.

Intermingled with each other's flesh, shot through with nails and screws, bits of rock, pieces of glass and broken marbles.

The plate glass windows of the pub across the street shatters from the concussion. Fragments of the glass knifed into the patrons. The number of casualties increased exponentially.

Walking up the street, the shockwave knocks June backward. She feels the heat of the blast wash over her. It takes away her breath as debris skitters around her.

June hears other people and wonders what language they are speaking. She can understand a few words of French and Spanish, but this is different. This is something else. Finnish? Basque?

June realizes – and the horror of it almost overcomes her and pulls her away from the lingering pain she feels from the blast – that people are crying and moaning and screaming.

June smells the searing of flesh and wood and plastics. To her left, across the street she sees a woman crawling along the wall, trying to stand, reaching for something to pull herself up. But the woman fails to find purchase on the brick wall and falls back to the sidewalk, pausing, then trying once again, not understanding that her hand is missing.

A pink bicycle clattering across the pavement, her rider spirited away.

A traffic light flashing red, green and yellow. in sequences seemingly random, but yet following a pattern as if its algorithm had been chased down and assassinated.

Vehicles stop at odd angles to each other and the geometry of the street.

A driver pushes open the door of his car, the window shattered. His face speckled with a pox that starts to bleed, slowly at first, then rushing down to soak his shirt.

There is a motion picture graininess to the scene that surrounds June and she wonders if her sight is impaired, as if the blast has destabilized her eyes, leeched all the color out of the night.

All her life June tried to learn the language of pain, to master its grammar. With a dozen tattoos and half as many piercings, she thought she had finally made sense of pain's syntax and vocabulary. But the blast was different. This was a new dialect for her, a true lingua franca of pain, universally understood.

THE HAGIOGRAPHY OF SONNY DRINKWATER

SCREAMING EVERYWHERE.

Screaming came, not across the sky, but echoing in the surf along Point Loma.

Screaming came in a wind running through the conifers of the North woods.

Screaming came pinwheeling along the horizon at sunset middle of the Indian Ocean.

Screaming came in a last gasp as the sailor slid down the serrated edge of coral waiting for the Great White to engulf him.

Screaming came while Sonny tweaked, when he most needed sleep, reminding him the whole world was one mad, screaming, paranoid rush of tweakers.

Screaming heard through broken teeth, from inside stolen tanks, within toxic clouds after trailer lab explosions.

Screaming howled when people decapitated their son and drove while talking to the lifeless head, secured beneath a seat belt on the passenger seat, teaching their child a final lesson.

Veterans swear they heard the screaming as Kamikaze pilots swept down in their Zeros.

Screaming heard whenever humans rush to the brink. And humans always rush to the brink

Screaming came for one more push, one more reach until everything, at last, goes over the edge.

Screaming where sea monsters wait and satellites loiter.

Screaming where rocket ships orbit and aliens swim among the supernovas

Screaming where airplanes dance with skyscrapers.

EVERYWHERE SCREAMING.

In the weeks after the two towers fell, Sonny Drink-water attempted to navigate the stench of ash and mingled lives snuffed out from a 10 inch square piece of double-paned glass he used to cut lines of crystal meth. During those weeks, Sonny kept the shades down and closed, the fresh fall air outside swept around his apartment, but never inside it, never cleaned out the smog of a meth binge.

When the crystal ran out and Sonny ventured outside, the city appeared the same. Traffic still sucked the life out of its drivers. The air tasted clean, but yet there was an aftertaste, a vestige of death and night and blood borne on westerly winds that sent the air of the towers up to Allston where it lingered, reminding everyone that this was where it had begun, where they had boarded the two planes. Then the winds dispersed the memory out to sea, out past Nova Scotia where it dissipated in the Gulf Stream east of Sable Island.

History has no meaning to men like Sonny. It passes them by. They pay it no attention, sitting, waiting for death to release them. In the end, Sonny created his own history. Yet there was no misguided notion of fame.

No desire to be somebody. He needed a hagiography of his own. The bomb was a reboot of that history.

When high, Sonny felt time no longer existed as the fourth dimension. Crank time transcended dimensions, traveled faster than light. It no longer seemed important to Sonny. What did it matter whether it was day or night when you had been awake for three days straight? In the Navy, Sonny waited for time to catch up. On watch, in sonar control, Sonny felt like Einstein dreaming about time, of trains lurching through deserted stations, about a sun that rises in the west and never sets, but lingers, held in place by gravity. On the fast frigate, always in danger of sailing too close to the edge of the world, the Earth kept going, accelerating and wobbling ever so slightly so that if Sonny stood in sonar control with only the blue lights on overhead and the scopes showing orange rills and Soviet submarines in the baffles, he thought he could sense this hurtling through space, the centrifugal forces at work, that shattering of gravity, instantaneous, but always repairable. Inside that blue-lit space of sonar control, Sonny traveled at 186,000 miles per second.

Let me tell you about the sea, Sonny said to his empty
apartment, his voided life,

Let me tell you about the sea,
The way the sky mutinies
and the stars shimmer
on a tattooed back.

Each ship lost in tropical
doldrums where cyclones form.
Is this the way to a bread fruit paradise?

While working aloft
under a white-knuckled sun,
I dream of inked daughters.

Let me tell you about the sea.
The way it mutinies against the sky
and washes away an aphotic night.

At sea, the ocean is silent. No birds chatter, the wind is free to pass unhindered, traffic does not linger, slouching over blacktop canals always heading back to the ocean like watersheds of commerce.

At sea, Sonny only heard the sounds of the frigate and the men, the dogging of doors, the air ducts, pots scraping on the messdeck, orders given, waves churning past the bow and the helicopter on the flight deck.

At sea, the ocean is all you can taste. Sonny savored it in the air, in the clouds, the sun and moon, in the swales between the waves, haloed around the stars, stars like so many methedrine crystals.

At sea, the ocean contained only one smell. Salt encrusted rails, salt when the sea monsters breech, salt when the silent sea slides past the rubber sonar dome, salt that you can't wash off your hands, wash out of your dungarees, scrape off your boondockers, salt in the food and the water and the coffee, black as a tattoo needle shading "homeward bound".

At sea, the ocean is constantly dropping off the edge of the world, as if the thin line of blackened horizon that pendulums with each roll of the ship was a *Fata Morgana* projecting images of islands and ships and breeching whales, but instead lured the ship deeper and deeper into a blue alien world just beyond the scope of her radar, beyond the reach of her sonar, getting closer and closer to the place where no human ears have heard the waves roll over and over as they have for millions of years.

At sea, the coal of a cigarette cupped in mid-air on the port bridge wing appears as just another star while the ship wedges through the ocean leaving a frothy glowing wake of bioluminescence.

At sea, the frigate becomes a moonless target on a dusty ocean, lost in a decaying orbit as if a tin can in space like a tin can at sea had slipped over the edge.

Crashing from the *plutonium* taste of meth, Sonny dreamt of people living in caves, returning to the surface crazy, the sun no longer comforting, the moon no longer holding any mystery and the stars. the people living in caves never recall the stars as if light pollution was all that remained and had become a secret language only they spoke.

Crashing from the *einsteinium* taste of meth, Sonny saw aircraft carriers bow down, helicopters drop out of the air, submerged ships struggle to the surface.

Crashing from the *californium* taste of meth, a blood puddle on the sands of Diego Garcia, blood like an electrical charge in Subic Bay, blood across two oceans calling sharks and sailors and sea monsters, blood shooting up the dropper's neck.

Sonny saw the dead and the weary clinging to a life raft, the inside of addiction and depression, poetry and music.

In his *Travelogue of Australia*, walking up from Circular Quay, Sonny saw sailors traffic in lies and tattoo the sky with debauchery. Sonny told a street walker in King's Cross he loved her. Jesus loves me, she said. Jesus loves you.

In his *Travelogue of Diego Garcia*, The Indian Ocean swallowed a shipmate. The coral glowed pink and yellow and came rushing up at Sonny's shipmate as he thrashed to reach the surface. So, this is it then. No more mid-watches on a ship at sea. No more evenings back home, the smell of butane and beef raked through the air. Sharks told the sailor their secrets as the sea spread summer clouds of blood.

Sonny said, we got high and bet on coconut crabs sprinting across crushed coral roads. He said there was time enough for sonar and ships and sharks. I heard, a shipmate said, that Great Whites won't bite you when you're drunk.

In his *Travelogue of Hong Kong*, from the top of Victoria Peak Sonny thought the city looked scrubbed clean, while drunk and freshly tattooed sailors off his fast frigate anchored in the middle of the harbor, lurched through the streets of the Wan-Chai where topless barmaids wear shawls because it's always winter inside the pubs.

In his *Travelogue of Korea*, Sonny felt helpless in the kimchee tinted smog, hungover on an ecological scale, reeling from spending the night with a girl in a room heated by a small coal brazier, her skin pure and blemish free, her black hair hooding and caressing his face when she hovered over him, smiling and laughing. All Sonny could see was the ocean in her eyes.

In his *Travelogue of Nagasaki*, on Sonny's ship, you could neither confirm nor deny the presence of nuclear weapons.

In the Nagasaki of Sonny's memory, in the Nagasaki
of his dreams, the plot varies little:

sounds of children playing and
birds singing drift through a park;
a bicyclist, delivering newspapers,
rides over the Megane Bridge;
a group of young women walk to
Mass at the Urakami Cathedral;
an elderly man, yoked with arthritis,
leans against a building and looks at his watch;
a trolley passes near the Torii Gate.

After the earth is scorched and the sky tastes like
metal and smells of burnt flesh, a tear in the atmosphere
mends, leaving a jagged scar and a polished black
monolith that reflects the shadows of the lucky ones.

From the top of Mt Laguna Sonny saw the earth stretching and twisting, working out a cramped muscle. Peyote coursing through the night sky, striated by the Milky Way leeching obscure knowledge, alien encounters and shipmates stranded on islands yet to be discovered – navigational maps referenced only deep sea volcanoes – where crystal pools of sweet blue liquid nourished the flora and fauna, where the cognoscenti tended interior vineyards and the hooligans, pedestrians and sailors argued essential questions of the universe and everyone on the frigate felt like Fletcher Christian.

During an acid trip, standing in the fog on one of the arms of the Ocean Beach pier, Sonny saw the growling faces of the living and dead, the end of the world and on the other side of the fog, far to the west, in the middle of a Pacific Ocean that defies gravity, as if it's floating out in space and unleashing yet more sea monsters, Sonny saw the ship sliding over the water to tropical islands and proxy wars, to sharks and submarines.

Sonny saw sheet lightning in the Philippines, snow at Ground Zero in Nagasaki, machine guns on street corners in Pusan, punk rock in Sydney, sharks in

Diego Garcia and thirty foot seas all across the ocean.
He heard the muezzin's call in Bahrain, felt the sands
from shamals on his skin like tiny birdshot.

The crew of the frigate hauled in all forward and aft lines and set a course deeper and deeper into an orphaned soul, to live on the treacherous sea in search of fleece and oil and wars of attrition. They laughed at the virgin deck hand wearing a battle helmet, standing in the prow, scanning the horizon for mail buoys and muttering into the 1MC, sweep down all decks, ladders and passageways.

Touch me gently, the ocean said.
But the frigate didn't listen.
Too late, the ocean said. Too late.
To starboard there rose leviathan, as if a convoy spirited out of the fog.
General Quarters!
All hands man your battle stations!
This is not a drill!

Allen Ginsberg said:
"Almost all our language is taxed by war."

But only the sea speaks of peace.

The sky of that perfect September day reminded Sonny of Diego Garcia. Of the two weeks the ship spent there just after the war ended. He had not seen a sky that blue when were they on patrol in the Persian Gulf. But there it was in Diego Garcia, cloudless, almost a weight too heavy to hang over the coral-rimmed atoll.

In the middle of the Pacific Ocean Sonny knew he sensed that the horizon was the end of the world. Sea monsters waited, or the ship would go pitch-poling over the edge into a blackness he only saw when he look over the side of the ship at night, the bioluminescence a jewel on that blackness.

The Indian Ocean was no different only there were white whales and the crew mustered no Ishmaels, Starbucks, Queequegs or Ahabs. The whale that did hit Sonny's ship near the Straits of Hormuz didn't stove her in, but only slid, impaled, down the bow to die, resting, on the sonar dome.

The crew of Sonny's ship didn't get a medal for rescuing the Vietnamese boat people crowded in a leaking, shattered scow in the South China Sea. They took them onboard and gave them blankets, water, food, medical attention. But the boat people were yesterday's news, cast off and cast away.

The crew of Sonny's ship did get a medal for rescuing Japanese fishermen off Samoa after their trawler sank. The crew spent a day and a half looking for heads floating in the water as if scanning for coconuts, wet, black-haired tips of icebergs, sharks feeding below, sun melting above. From a crew of sixteen Sonny and his shipmates pulled less than half out of the ocean.

For that they gave the crew a medal.

Sonny turns the television off. He has already seen the towers fall over and over. That perfect day when Sonny thought he was someone else, someone good blurred into a beautiful evening. The sky so clear that the sun set instantly. There were no lingering colors, only a grainy black partly devoured by light pollution. If there were stars that night, Sonny did not bother to look.

Crashing from the *promethium* taste of meth, Sonny becomes ocean, becomes death, becomes man plundering the pit.

Crashing from the *mendelevium* taste of meth, Sonny becomes sea monster, becomes blazing comet, becomes suicide visionary.

Crashing from the *seaborgium* taste of meth, Sonny becomes chaotic good, becomes trickster, becomes rocket ship.

Crashing from the *nihonium* taste of meth, Sonny becomes shipwrecked, becomes lost at sea, becomes castaway in paradise.

Crashing from the *uranium* taste of meth, Sonny becomes a small cold part of the solar system, becomes somnambular, becomes pregnant with *nihonium*, with *platinum* and *kryptonite*.

Crashing from the *chromium* taste of meth,
Sonny becomes a wind

in maples,
pin cherry,
beech and birch
that sounds like a ship
bow down
in rough seas

Crashing from the *titanium* taste of meth,
Sonny becomes a heave of

green water
washing the leaves,
and then a silence,
curtained,
as if drowning.

Searching on the Internet, Sonny finds ingredient lists and recipes for pressure cookers, timers and hydrogen peroxide. He buys nails, wire staples for wiring, a hammer and a box of marbles. Sonny smashes the marbles into pieces on the floor of his apartment, breaks beer bottles and stirs the nails and staples into a deathly batter.

THE TATTOOS OF JUNE AND ÖTZI

June dreams about Ötzi the iceman and black rills in his skin. Tattoos to combat arthritis, talismans against transmogrified evil spirits, three lines on parchment-like skin, and the shadowed history of humans rubbing red ochre on the bodies of their dead, of pushing dye into skin with oak needles. Long before humans painted on the walls of caves, skin was the first canvas artists worked on.

Find my killer, Ötzi, the iceman said.

But I want to tattoo you, June said. I want to feel inside your fur hat and wear your leggings. I want to kiss the rabbet left behind by the arrow that killed you.

Find my killer. That's all I ask, Ötzi said.

But we could circumnavigate the universe, become cartographers of each other's bodies. Spend languorous afternoons under an equatorial sun.

I'll give you berries and nuts if you find my killer.

Before I find your killer, I want to find out why he tracked you and chased you up that mountain. Where did you live? Who did you offend or trespass against? What gods did you worship?

When you find my killer, Ötzi said, you'll know the truth. Until then I'll remain an enigma, a code to be broken, an amorphous black hole of unmatched DNA and longing.

June sports bird effigies over her breasts: a redwing blackbird over the left and an evening grosbeak over her right. Flowerless rose vines crawl from her pubic mound and spiral across her stomach and around her navel, punctuated with a Rimbaud quote *I'm intact, and I don't give a damn.* On each arm, Celtic-style snakes reach from the tops of her hands and wrap around the length of the arm to her shoulders. A Salish Indian design, the Cowichan Crest, remains unfinished on her back, only the outline of the thunderbird carrying the orca is visible. On the outside of her thighs, swim Micronesian dolphins.

June set out to fill a vacuum in her life with ink. She found books and magazines with photographs of tattoos. There were red and raw devil faces surrounding shaved vulvas, noses the length of flaccid penises, portraits of dead rock stars on forearms, great weeping Christ effigies on backs, petroglyphs dancing like a crown around a shaved skull and the samurai warriors, dragons and koi fish of the Japanese full body tattoo. The emptiness that June felt was the emptiness a clean canvas might feel waiting for the caress of an artist's brush. She knew she could never use religion to fill that emptiness. She had tried drugs in high school, but found they made her feel stupid and out of control. She liked an order to everything and thought underachieving was overrated. During college, she had used sex to fill the emptiness. Those encounters, with dumb handsome boys only created parallel universes of emptiness. She had never liked their clumsy fingers, the way they reached for her, squeezed her, tested to see if she were ready.

After each desperate encounter with dumb handsome boys, June rewarded herself with a tattoo and redesigned her body. She started slowly and secretly. A crescent moon above the ankle, a thin ribbon of triangles across her wrist, easily hidden under a watch or bracelet.

June dreams of kissing Ötzi's mouth. Her identity is in his mouth. She kisses him all night. Her breath grows inside him, filling him with her, bringing him back to life. June tastes the truth on Ötzi's lips. She knows there is history in Ötzi's eyes. If only Ötzi remembered what color were June's eyes, darkened at night like the moon reflected in the ocean, splitting into two moons, three moons, four moons, then returning to one moon. Silver and black.

In a world where time starts and stops, but never pauses, never lets one rewind and try again, in that world, Ötzi told his brother one night as they watched their shared world darken, I do not exist.

In this world where he did not exist Ötzi imagines himself on a planet with violent weather. Across the face of this world storms rise up, grow, and sweep over the land and sea. Thousands of electrical charges dash from the energized clouds to the sodden soil every second. Great waves on the ocean expand, pushing inland and smashing everything in their way.

Ötzi imagines himself on this planet struggling to find reason in the madness of the weather. Whichever way he turns the weather assaults him. The sky clears and the land dries and the ocean shrinks back to its normal placid state, the yellow star above burns and parches Ötzi, blistering his skin.

Ötzi imagines himself on this planet trying to master the weather. Then June arrives to share her world with him, to share her kisses, to share her tattoos.

June wants to write a hagiography of Magellan with Ötzi. He doesn't understand and only wants to kiss her.

We could stand in the middle of the road and build a house together, June said, or, we could drive to the shore and see where the ocean carries us.

We could hop a freight to McDonalds, June said, and dip our fries in a strawberry shake and wait for the waves to wash away the parking lot and carry us back down the tracks. We could read new books and burn the old ones, June said, and from the ashes of this bonfire of vocabularies mix a new ink on new paper.

We could block out the sun, magnify the moon, June said, or estimate the day and hour and minute when the Hadron Collider rips gravity out of space and restores balance to the tides.

We could, June said, stand in the middle of the road and, like Magellan before us, circumnavigate our world just by touching fingers and lips.

We should, Ötzi said.

Velikovsky believes, June said between sips of coffee, *that Venus, once captured in orbit by the Sun, wreaked havoc upon the Earth, plunging us into darkness and terror.*

They were in a small cafe somewhere in Montmartre chasing ghosts and the bleeding edge of art, science and desire.

Venus parted seas, rained a nourishing nectar upon the earth and made the sun rise in the east and set in the west where once the opposite was true, she said. They walked up to Square Louis Michel, holding hands. *Paris' birth, like Venus' was written in bloodshed that continues today,* June said.

Ötzi did not want to believe it. Could not. Even as bombs went off and his synapses became like controlled avalanches.

Ötzi left history behind for the rubbery folds of June's labia. He tugged at one of her piercings and she gasped.

We are. Being. Lied to, she said.

Ötzi wanted to rewrite the laws of gravity, to explore quantum mechanics, to catalog the chaotic history of the Higgs Bosun Archipelago, but June wanted only to create her own truth, a long Darwinian slide back to the sea, to yonic perfection.

Do historians know the lies they write, June said. You're no better than a medieval hagiographer of saint's lives. Velikovsky knew the truth about Venus. Velikovsky knew the historian, like the journalist that files phony bylines, was better at exploring the back of his own hand than the thoughts and feelings of people one hundred, two hundred or a thousand years before. Herodotus, Flavius Josephus, Joe Gould, Wells' ridiculous Outline of History *or Van Loon and his unintentional attempts at humor, everything they know is wrong.*

When Ötzi pressed her for the truth, she smiled and kissed him.

On the last day Ötzi saw June in Paris, he was writing a history of his travels, of facts and figures, quotations and anecdotes held together by gluey bits of gravity, plagiarizing false forensics like a party boss buying votes. Ötzi had cities to describe to distant rulers, but all that was cut short and he ended up on that mountain, his manuscript unfinished and undiscovered until June found it in his tattoos.

The sun leeched blood across the earth and Venus promised a new day. How that star came to shine in our sky was a secret history that none dare reveal. June knew its truth, but she only hinted at it and whispered that Newton was a charlatan. Then she kissed Ötzi and he never saw her again until they ran into each at the Y.

June told Ötzi she liked swimmng with him.

Those fat old Russians, she said, *they're all over the lane and always rubbing up against me.*

They do the same to me, Ötzi said.

The Russian men in the pool are not headhunters, but the Chinese men share mysteries with the other swimmers as if they are all diving for copies of Mao's *Little Red Book.*

What was the worst thing you ever did? June asked Ötzi.

I can't tell you, he said.

Who killed you? June said.

What was the worst thing you ever did?, Ötzi said.

I once held my sister's head under water at a lake. She nearly drowned. She got an ear infection and now she's deaf in her left ear.

Is that why you like to swim?

I'm a good swimmer, June said.

If history is promoted as entertainment, then we could say June's story is true. It certainly is a terrible thing to do, even for children. But perhaps, the real truth lies in between the words June chose to tell her story. Therein lies history's ability to adapt.

The truth is that June's sister saved her from drowning. When she was little June loved to swim. She had been taught not to fear the water, but to master it. Still, when her leg cramped and turned to a stone that was slowly crushing the air out of her lungs as she sank to the bottom of the lake she felt the water filling her lungs. She wanted to scream. June could no longer see the sky above her; the black water was pushing down into her. The ache in her lungs mimicked the ache in her leg. Before the last bubble of air leaked out of her, her sister pulled June up to the surface and dog-paddled back to the shore with her.

If drowning is so peaceful, she would ask friends, then why did my whole body ache? Why did it feel like I was being crushed? They could not answer her. They did not know what it felt like to drown. Instead of answering the questions, they would say that they would rather drown than die in a fire.

The Hànzi characters inked on June's side told Ötzi less about her than the way she swam, training for an open water competition. She high-fived him after he swam a lap of butterfly and thanked him for his military service. He was never in the military, but he had been in a war and ended up on that mountain where they would find abandoned soldiers from the Great War. He didn't want to be thanked. He wanted a kiss, a grilled cheese sandwich with a tomato slice, a glass of iced tea with no lemon or sugar. He wanted to touch June the way the ocean touched her.

On a perfect planet, Ötzi and June leave the pool and drive into the dark American night.

On a perfect planet, Ötzi and June find desiccated road side memorials

On a perfect planet, Ötzi and June stop at each memorial and invent histories for the deaths.

On a perfect planet, Ötzi and June finger the plastic flowers, the crosses, the paraphernalia of bikers and hippies, of families, mothers and fathers, classmates. Scattered around the sites are moldy cigarette packs, crushed beer cans, t-shirts, jeans, underwear, ballcaps with frayed bills resembling an upside U. Tacked to the nearby trees, telephone poles, or taped to crumbled and cauterized walls are weathered poems scribbled on yellow legal paper.

Who are these victims? How did they die?

The mother coming down the hill too fast into a grove of trees.

The biker chick head-on in the fog.

The drunk friend talking a turn too sharply.

The pick-up demolished by a semi-tractor trailer at the intersection of a farm road and a state highway.

The double suicide off a bridge. Did they hold hands going down? Did one instantly regret the jump, the other gleeful and relieved?

On this perfect planet, Ötzi and June drive the crumbling US highways, the state highways and county roads. They stay off the interstates.

No hitchhikers, pedestrians, scooters and horseback riding.

The interstates lull you into sense of security where safety and speed cohabit, but ultimately, the real world would break in: a tractor trailer fishtailing, black ice sending a school bus plummeting down an embankment, a confused elderly couple entering the highway in the wrong direction, the many drunk drivers that pollute the roads.

On this perfect planet, Ötzi and June eat at diners and roadside grills with Reuben sandwiches and potato chips in small airless bags.

On this perfect planet, Ötzi and June scan for the birdhouse makers, the gourd growers and the Emu farmers. Hedgehogs scurry along the road. A fox dashes out in front of them, but just as suddenly darts back to safety. At dusk, a family of deer, wet from a fresh downpour, run along the grassy shoulder and leap back into the darkening woods. Heron rise out of the marshes. Cranes, their skyscraper heads above the cattails, strain in silence for a fish in the swamp.

On this perfect planet, Ötzi and June do not expect the end of the road. They don't care if they make it to Alaska or Florida or both.

On this perfect planet, Ötzi and June camp, sleep in neon-lit motel when they need showers. In the motels June moves beyond the three lines when she tattoos Ötzi. The tattoos are foreplay.
The tattoos become Ötzi's diary of the trip.

On this perfect planet, June wants the turquoise ankle bracelets from the Navajos selling in stalls at Four Corners. She want the pronghorn deer to smile at her, the corralled buffalo to roam freely. She wants the hawks, eagles and turkey vultures to circle over the van and follow it as if they were dolphin escorting a boat. She wants the continent to be her home and drive every winding mile, every hairpin turn and every dangerous rockslide area. She wants to cross all the rivers: the Connecticut, the Hudson, the Alleghany, the Mississippi, the Missouri, the Canadian and the Platte. Where the watersheds divide, splitting the continent into bite sized portions, they stop and feel the oceans tugging apart the land. In the Adirondacks where the Hudson and the Mohawk flow to the Atlantic and the Black and the Grass flow to the St. Lawrence; in the Rockies where the Missouri flows to the Mississippi and the Snake flows to the Pacific and the Green flows to the Colorado, they stop and feel and taste and smell geology.

June wants to know the magic of America as the natives knew it: the power of Devil's Tower, of Mt. Shasta, and ultimately of Denali.

June wants all the Frank Lloyd Wright buildings to last forever. She wants to live in Falling Water, use Taliesin as an office and Taliesin West as a winter retreat.

On this perfect planet, June wants Carhenge, Route 66 and the Snowflake Motel preserved. She wants towering statues of Paul Bunyan and Babe, Hiawatha, little Paul and Paul's anonymous wife with the C-section scar.

How else could she give birth to such a giant?

June wants Wall Drug, and Crazy Horse carved in to a mountain. She wants Petrified Creatures and Petrified Forests. She wants rocks and fossils on the coast of Nova Scotia and Viking settlements in Newfoundland.

June wants the cities and the pollution and the heat and cold; the snows and the hurricanes, the tornadoes and the droughts. She wants the trees, the strip mines, the dams, the lakes, and the salmon to spawn again. She wants animals to stay away from the road.

June wants America as the Natives first found it. She wants wooly mammoths and saber-tooth tigers. She wants to watch the sun set on the Great Plains, turn around and watch the moon rise at the same time. June wants a red sky at night and a red sky in morning.

But most of all, on this perfect planet, June wants to feel Ötzi. She wants this dream of Ötzi to never end.

June does not believe in divine retribution, paranormal activity or seismic disturbances. She wants to hear the coda clicks of a sperm whale. At night, in the city, she searches the sky for the shoulder of Orion, but only sees his belt. The Seven Sisters remains an erased smudge of white chalk. If June dove with them, the whales could see the stars in her eyes.

SMOKEY OF THE MIGRAINES

Smokey and Lefty are down the union hall talking to Sully. They want no shows. They want Sully to pay up, Sully to arrange for Lefty's brother-in-law to work. Sully can't do it. Smokey says to him he says you can't or won't you bastard. Smokey sees Sully ain't going to oblige them ain't playing along. No matter the reason Smokey don't like people who can't or won't. Smokey don't find their recalcitrance funny. Lefty looks longways – his mouth is always drooping – when Smokey says recalcitrance. Where'd ya learn that, Lefty says. Father Xavier. He says to me he says ya know Smokey your boys, the boys you sent me last week they wouldn't kneel and pray with me, pray on the hard floor of the rectory mudroom. ten Hail Marys, an Act of Contrition nothing difficult nothing no Catholic boy growing up in the projects couldn't recite after confession. Recalcitrant they was Smokey he says to me. Lefty don't care what a pedophile junkie says, the pervert fucker. He wants a job for the bastard his sister married that no good half Irish dipshit. At least he ain't no dagowop bastard Lefty had whispered to his mother at the wedding. But now this jerk, this recalcitrant Sully ain't letting go of what he has, of what he owes and Smokey's not haven't it.

Lefty senses it.
Lefty tastes it.
Lefty feels it.

Heat and steam curdling off the nicotine stained drop ceiling. Lefty knows if Smokey don't act soon, don't kill this fucker leave his body in the mud of the bay then Smokey's migraine's gonna go supernova.

Lefty smells it.

Sulfur, sparks, ozone coming off Smokey. The migraine's burning inside Smokey's head. All the dead light in the room, the murdered light, shatters at the edge of Smokey's visible spectrum. Sully's whiny voice pile drives deeper into Smokey's head. Outside, a commuter train whistle blows and rattles the windows. The migraine takes Smokey outside his body where he exists far from the reach of life, of love, beyond the polished black metal of the Glock 9 he shoves in Sully's mouth, chipping a tooth and cutting the fucker's lips. Smokey smells the piss soaking Sully's pants. The migraine gets Smokey thinking of every mother fucker who thought he knew better, who wouldn't give up what he owed. Why does every fuckhead think he can do what he wants, hold on to what he owes, what he's obligated to give up whether its jobs or money, drugs or pussy. The migraines speak to Smokey in tongues he barely understands. They tell him stories that have no meaning. The migraines talk at him in incomprehensible words.

The migraine is a ghost whispering of death and night and blood. The migraine is severing occipital nerves with electricity. The migraine is a creature living in Smokey's neck reaching up through his brain and pulling each eye back back down. The migraine is an itch beneath the straps of a back pack straining with the weight of its terrible truth, of nails and screws, bits of rock, pieces of glass and broken marbles. The migraine is smoke and burnt flesh, burnt wood, burnt plastic, as if a scream had a smell, a taste, a touch. The migraine is the splatter of paint, an ocular darkness of color and sound. The migraine is the mortification of flesh glazed with auras and sounds heard rumbling under the skin, rifling through marrow. The migraine is a killing field, manured with the blood of shell-shocked men.

The migraine exists outside ecclesiastical boundaries, a leftover of Purgatory, lingering to plague the unholy, the lost ones who left the Church or turned away from the light.

Smokey can't seek the light because
the migraine is light,
diffused, catholic, exquisite
as if the blue of Smokey's irises is a laceration.

Smokey hesitates, a coronal hammer, a brief pause, a shadow on his grave, like glaciers stopped at the edge of the continent, like the planet shifting, like the tides frozen between migraines and screaming. In that pause, that hesitation Smokey knows there exists all the time he needs for him to get back in the car and drive back through the tolls, back to an ocular hell of pain and auras and screaming that is the migraine, to drive back to the edge of the bridge, back to a slow suicide, an invisible, inevitable slide to death as if the jump off the bridge was horizontal and took years to complete, where only the screaming remained, burning, as if the migraine had caught fire and the ferric smell of blood, was a weight too heavy to hang over a city where no planes scream like rockets, where no alarms sound, where no firefighters climb a thousand stairs, where no bodies fall and hit the concrete ground like so many bundles of 2x4's, where no buildings collapse or rip apart, where fragments of glass do not ink the sky with a freighted penmanship, where no vans cartwheel through pedestrians, set adrift in a solar system searching for life, where no colors, leeched out of the night, become ligaments of memory, of sacrifice, of lost time, where no weddings or buses or marathons, varnished with a wicked wind, disappear into the maw of gravity, where there are no paintings to finish, no poems to write, no sound tracks to compose, where Smokey is no longer haunted by the polluted soil and withered by the cold winds of a city on a hill; in that pause, that hesitation before the trigger is pulled, before the button is pushed, before the boxcutter is swung, before the dustbin of history is emptied, before the punks and anarchists and situationists spell the word:

s·p·e·c·t·a·c·l·e

a filtered signal darkens the edges of Smokey's senses, each shutting down except the screaming, the migraine still alive, the stars still pinwheeling above in the murkiness of a blackhole where Smokey, at last, understands the nature of time. But Smokey can't squeeze his head the way he likes when he's home in bed, pressing his palms into each temple like the book press that Uncle Fester used to cure his headaches on *The Addam's Family*. All the kids laughed at that. But Smokey knew it worked, knew it helped shut out the explosions that threatened to overwhelm him, threatened to send him down a pit where only pain and nausea and fire and eternal damnation waited. Smokey don't notice he's lost in the migraine, time traveling, to Dealey Plaza where the sun never sets for the king returned, for the king sacrificed, for the king kissing his boots, the Book Depository a new capitol, and the hundred years between two kings and the letters of their names, the mountain ranges, latitudes and assassins. *Sic semper tyrannis!* Smokey time-traveling through the migraine, through ropes of light, to Marat's bath, water on the tile, footsteps in the hall, a ghost, a shadow, an angel, an assassin, always assassins, the knife drinking blood. *J'ai tué un homme!* I killed one man to save thousands! Smokey time traveling to the shabby Mexico City room Trotsky called home, to Constantinople when the sun bled, to the end of a dusty alley in Ojinaga where the old Gringo, the old *viejo loco* had come to meddle, to exorcise the ghosts of Shiloh, where dust haloed his eyes and words kept spilling out of the holes in his chest, where his blood was tattooed with the bitter dust of Villa's revolution, a glorious lost cause chased across the desert. Villa, who would never ride to rescue Smokey, who would never escape the barking dogs, and gunshots, and dead horses, the frugality of a canister shot cutting down whole platoons, the dust of war. At the birth of Mary Shelley's monster Smokey stood and shook with recognition knowing only ice and madness. Smokey urged the Beothuk to push Leif Erickson back into the sea. He watched men attain the knowledge of gods and burn holes in the sky over White Sands, Hiroshima, Nagasaki and Bikini. Smokey armed Metacom and counseled him to raze New England, knowing the Pokanoket would eventually lose. Tituba created poultices for Smokey's migraines, for the fear, for the devils of Salem. In the attic on Kennedy's farm – again the king – Smokey watched John Brown hand out pikes to his men, telling them they were about to do the Lord's work. Smokey's with Traven during the cruel, joyous summer of 1914, before the desiccated landscapes of France, before the archaeology of mud and blood and the gristle of men snuffed out in the *frontgraben*, before the dead right eye of migraines, the dashed skulls, the rats and the little corporal, the ocular migraine hanging on the wire, trussed up as if a crucifixion and the green glazing of gas were a defense against mutiny and yet more migraines. Smokey's with Traven digging skull fragments out of the ruins of Verdun, a boot with toe bones from the banks of the Marne, a punctured helmet in the woods near Charlevaux. Smokey's back with the witch at Topsfield Fair who told him he had the longest life line she had ever seen. That was when Smokey started to believe he couldn't be touched, that bullets would pass through him and the Feds would look the other way while he and Lefty raked it in. Smokey says to Sully, he says I can't be touched. I am un fucking touchable you hear me you fucking fuck motherfucker. The migraine needs more than a long life line, it needs pressure, it needs quiet and darkness, it needs salvation. Smokey once asked Father Xavier whether the migraines were penance, punishment from God for Smokey's sins, for turning a blind eye to the priest's preying on the lost boys from the projects, for the shots of smack he gave the priest whenever Father Xavier came back from Suffolk Downs broke and dejected, straying from the protection of Mary the Mother of God. Smokey wonders if he might find salvation in the migraines after all. Free the pain, do penance for all the killings, for letting the Feds take Johnny Longneck and for sticking his gun in Mairead's cunt after she slapped his face. A migraine won't change the sound mud makes when it sucks a body in with a watery gasp. Smokey always liked that sound, amazed the mud acted like a vacuum as if the mud had become a gate to a ghost city, a city of cow paths and witches, and the torments of hell, a city of oceans and pirates, mutineers, red Indians, praying Indians, a city founded on a catechism of catastrophe. In that city, in the clam flats, on the shores of drumlins and rivers that turn in on themselves, the Feds'd need back-hoes to dig up, from the oily muck, the bones of Smokey's migraines. When we kill this fuck, Smokey says to Lefty, he can't go in where everyone else is. Don't want people to think we're lazy or dumb or something. We can run him out to sea. Go fish for cod off Nova Scotia. Why not smuggle him into Nova Scotia. Guns, drugs and bodies, a smuggler can handle anything just like a salesmen should be able to sell anything, like a man of the cloth can absolve the sins of murderers, thieves and housewives all on the same day. Each sinner says an Act of Contrition. Each ready and willing to commit more sins. No absolution, no dispensation, no sin eaters can cure a migraine. Smokey feels nauseous, his skin paper white, but his hand steady. All his other senses shuddering and shaking. The florescent lights bleeding through the migraine, skinning and scraping the inside of Smokey's skull, wire-brushing his eyes. Sully whimpering, sees no flashes of his life, offers no regrets, knows no need to apologize. The Glock, now full of blood and spit tastes like a rosary, like salvation, like the red wine of Christ's blood as if the gun is pure and transmogrified. The ocean, just over the Expressway, is a luxury, a monastery of islands in the bay, drumlins rising up from the clam beds and mud flats and beaches of torpedoed glass, shells, rusted rafts and submarine nets. How many miles to Nova Scotia,

Smokey says. Lefty shrugs his shoulders, far enough, he says. Far enough for this fuck to feed the sharks, far enough to the edge of the continent, to the edge of the world, far enough for this fuck to feed all the sea monsters and white whales, far enough for drowned sailors trapped in Davy Jones' Locker far enough for Shellbacks, far enough for shipwrecks and cannibals, far enough for the migraine.

The migraine is a 9mm under Smokey's pillow.

The migraine is the guts of a burner phone on the floor.

The migraine is a whiskey bottle on the nightstand.

The migraine is a dream, a nightmare become blackness, as if Smokey, falling out buildings on fire, on a planet with violent weather full of electrical charges, and oceans painting the land black, had discovered burning stars, solar flares and migrainous caverns.

The migraine is a fall from grace.

The migraine is Smokey's sister left for dead, a needle in her arm, behind the old fire station, young boys poking sticks at her, trying to wake her, testing their knowledge of science and God in a city under a bridge, an Indian village with clear, cold spring water turned foul, polluted with oil farms and turpentine, and varnishes, and tankers, and drawbridges, and war, and burning frigates.

The migraine is a rag shop fire, a conflagration charring a city, turning black the sides of buildings, back porches, parlors, and during supper, the faces of children and mothers and grandmothers.

The migraine is a vision.

The migraine is vision.

The migraine exists without color.

The migraine is a vocabulary without words,
without sounds.

The migraine is a revolution, a manifesto of pain.

The migraine is a running sea,
a *Fata Morgana*, an ocular horizon.

The bullet shatters the back of Sully's coruscating head.

The migraine is Smokey.

A REQUIEM FOR LEFTY

Once, after his first stint in prison, Lefty went to a psychic known for her expertise in past lives. When he walked in the door of her home office, she told him to stop and not come in any further. There's a shadow on you, she said. They're corrosive, like acid at the corners of your eyes. You have experienced too much pain and suffering. If you can hold out in this life, to treat others kindly, you might be released from the demon's torment.

After he left the psychic, he bought heroin for the first time and hoped his release would come quickly. The heroin dulled the edges, settled the anxiety he felt from knowing he had spirits crouching in his shadow. Who wants spirits anywhere near them. When he stood in the sun he looked down to see what colors his shadows had become. With heroin, Lefty's shadow spirits became a dull gray, their urgency leeched out and spilled across the ground.

Lefty fills three 15-shot magazine clips for the Beretta 9mm he bought off a *paisano* he had met in MCI Concord. Lefty remembers the guy had 'The Ave' tattooed on his stomach. Lefty hates that style, that old English lettering. You can't hardly read the words.

Lefty did not trust the Italian kid. They met in the park opposite the police station. Both laughed at that. Neither laughed easily these days.

The Beretta 9mm offers a variety of tactical features that make it equally safe, easy to use and dependable in the holster of military personnel as well as for home or personal defense. Its reversible magazine release lets you use either hand for tactical magazine changes, while its ambidextrous safety-decocker makes it flexible for right- or left-handed persons or for shooters trying out different gripping or shooting styles.
— Beretta Sale Sheet

Sitting at the red formica kitchen table Lefty cleans the Beretta while looking out the window. The triple-deckers across the street hide secrets. Their brown exteriors line the small street like a canyon wall. Lefty feels comfortable, feels at home in the studio apartment; in the same shabby building his grandparents had lived. God rest their souls, he signs a cross. They had died while he did his first time in prison. Stupid kid stuff. Stolen car with a trunkload of drugs. He got off easy. First offense. 3 to 5 in MCI-Concord. Nineteen years old, long hair, cute boy face with peach fuzz on his lip. After the first rape attempt he made a shiv. Trust no one. He learned it well.

When he got out his cousin Smokey told him one thing.

Trust no one but me, he said.

Trust no one but me.

Especially don't trust Shawmut.

But here he was back in Shawmut.

The city calls him every time he gets out.

Shawmut, with its history of burning.

Shawmut by the sea.

Shawmut, the Indian village long destroyed, filled with toxins and oil farms and gas tanks and crumbling wharves lining the black polluted river, Shawmut Creek. The river so narrow that the Shawmut class of tanker ship was named after it. The drawbridges to East Allston were always damaged from tankers sliding past and scraping, or banging the bridgework.

Shawmut of the three hills, each rising above the triple-deckers and the decayed factories. The hospital at the top of Mount Bellingham where Lefty was born now gone, replaced by low-income housing. The Soldier's Home atop Powderhorn Hill operated as a rest home for the elderly. They built condos on the slopes of Admirals Hill and turned the Naval Hospital at its summit into a luxury apartment building. Lefty's great-uncle had died at the Naval Hospital from wounds he suffered when his ship was sunk in the North Atlantic. Shawmut under the bridge. Shawmut covered in soot and shadow and noise.

Shawmut of the renewal, the false promises and the new schools and the state receivership and the illegal gambling clubs and the prostitution rings and the crack factories and the fires.

Always the fires.

Shawmut of the great fires.

The first fire, in 1908, started in the rag shops, where the Jewish immigrants from Russian pogroms and Central European poverty came to make it rich. The Poles, the Irish and the French Canadians came later. The fire burned a fire station, one fourth of the city and killed hundreds of immigrants. The second great fire started on October 14, 1973 at Arlington and Third Streets, in the crumbling shops and hazardous chemical warehouses built after the first Great Shawmut Fire. Fifteen hundred men took four days to bring the fire under control. It burned one third of the city, the last great urban renewal event. It took years for the rebuilding.

Shawmut was lost and now it was found.

Lefty remembered the second fire. He watched Smokey and that other kid, Frenchy, light the fire. The three of them watched it spread and grow and suck in oxygen. They felt the air collapse and rush forward down the narrow streets. It jumped from Third Street to Second Street and back across to Everett Avenue, from Arlington Street to Carter Street, to Spruce Street where the flames caressed the bridge.

On the day of the Great Fire something snapped inside Lefty. He remembered feeling excited by the spread of the fire. Thinking that he could get away with anything.

Lefty lights another cigarette, stands up, Lefty tucks the Beretta in the waist of his jeans and the two extra magazine clips in his pockets. He buttons a flannel shirt and lets the tail hang down, covering the slight bulge at his waist. Smoke from the cigarette curls into his eyes. He squints, rolling up the sleeves of the shirt to his biceps. India inked tattoos cover both arms. On the left, a snake curls from out of the sleeve, around the forearm, its head resting on the top of the hand. On the right, crosses and swastikas dance every time Lefty turns his wrist. He looks in the bathroom mirror and combs the crew cut with his fingers. The jagged scar from his mouth up the left cheek to under his eye looks, to him, like a highway from hell. The scar makes his mouth droop even more to the left. He will never forget the fight with the white guy, a drug dealing, greaser, long haired smart alec. Lefty rattles the slurs off in his head. Fuck him. He touches the scar and examines the crow's feet around his eyes and the gray hairs on his temple. He's too old for this shit.

Beretta Model – 92FS
Barrel Length – 4.9"
Overall Length – 8.5"
Weight Unloaded – 33.3 oz
Frame Size – Full Size
Activity – Defense
Caliber – 9X19 (PARA)
Action – Double/Single
Overall Height – 5.4"
Overall Width – 1.5"
Family – 92FS
Firearm Type – Pistol
Product Segment – Home Defense
Magazine Capacity – 15 Rounds
— Beretta Spec Sheet

Outside, an east wind, thick with exhaust and jet fuel from Logan, lifts traces of the ocean up and inland. The air covers East Allston, Everett and Shawmut in a cancerous blanket. The three cities are industrial wastelands where the poorest of the poor lived. The citizens shamble down the blackened streets while the rain drops poison on their heads, burning holes into their skin. There is always talk of expanding the airport. Where? Lefty didn't care. He knew when they used runway two-seven. On approach the jets flew over his building.

When he arrives at the park opposite the police station he sits on a bench and looks at the yellow crumbling building. He is early. He has all the time in the world.

William Burroughs once said the only time a junkie knew was junk time.

Cop. Shoot. Cop.

Time is no longer important to Lefty. He sits and waits for time to stop. At Cedar Junction he waited for time. They all waited for time in lockdown. There was nothing else but time. In lockdown you never see the sun set or rise, never witness a cloud passing across the sun, that sudden change from brilliance to a cooling translucence. In lockdown the lights are always on. Inside is a penal experiment in time, where the system uses time as a form of punishment. There is no contemplation of right or wrong, of evil and good, but only of truth and untruth, of time that sits like a shadow in the cell waiting for mercy, waiting for release whether it comes in the form of death or parole. For Lefty, the choice never mattered.

Sitting on the bench in the small dusty park of brick pathways and flowerbeds full of dying plants, Lefty wonders whether he has that gene that predisposes a person to crime. Did the shape of his skull lead him to a life of crime? Did distance between his eyes lead him to sitting in this park across from a police station with a hand gun tucked in his pants?

Lefty smokes a cigarette and watches police officers entering and leaving the station.

Lefty flips the cigarette butt away, crosses the street and enters the police station.

This is it. This is everything his life has become. Before Smokey went on the lam, Lefty would never have considered doing this. But with Smokey gone, there was nothing more Lefty could do. He had done too much time. He pulls the 9mm out of his pants and shoots.

The cop at the desk stands and falls. Two more cops fall. The cop holding a Hispanic man turns. Lefty recognizes him. He remembers Frenchy when they were kids playing ringolevio. He remembers Frenchy beating him up because Lefty wouldn't smoke a cigarette. He remembers Frenchy lighting fires because his dad was a fire fighter. *Only way I can see my old man,* Frenchy told him. But memories don't mean shit and Lefty knows this and shoots at Frenchy, hitting the Hispanic man instead.

Ejecting the empty clip, Lefty takes a fraction too long to pop a full one in. Before he can continue shooting, Frenchy shoots him six times in the chest.

Lefty smells the blood and
sees lights flashing and
shimmering and
stars pinwheeling and
the weather turning and
a blazing black flame furrowing
under his shirt where the blood
whispers his real name and
Smokey's name and
Frenchy's name and
the names of everyone they killed and
finally, the names of the spirits
the palmist said crouched in his shadow.
Lefty wonders if this is what Smokey
sees when he gets a migraine.

Lefty wonders what Smokey would do.

The last day Lefty seen his cousin Smokey, Lefty said: *Member how the big kids yousta palm us quarters so they could use our bikes to do drug runs? There was that skinny rat faced one. Mulcahy, I think. Once, he gave me his driver's license as collateral, I guess. If he don't come back with my bike fuck I'm going to do with his license. When he came back with my bike, he says, it's expired ya know. I'm like, what, what's expired. He says, my ID, my license is expired. Still, I can't figure out what the fuck this rat face is telling me. A license is a license right. Then he says, he'll be back the next day and is gonna gimme a buck instead, but not the license. Never shows back up. Dead, in jail. I don't know and I'm thinking I don't really care. He was just some rat face who gave me money so he could use my bike to buy drugs. A few months later we were driving back from visiting my grandparents and there's the rat face with a couple of other sketchy looking guys hanging out in front of Hy's drugstore. One of the guy's got a mohawk and I member thinking how cool is that. My father says, that's Mark Mulcahy's son. Guess he's out on bail for drug possession. My father calls him a scumbag. Me, being stupid, says he used to give me money to use my bike. I don't* know any better. What were we like maybe ten. My dad turns around gives me a good crack on the mouth. Not the worst he ever did, but fuck that one hurt like a bastard. He had that paratroopers ring on his finger.

This is how Lefty leaves the 21st Century. With a memory in orbital decay, until there was nothing left, a seemingly pleasant dream filtered out until a thin line black appeared and like that old tv signal, popped and was gone.

THE CITY UNDER THE BRIDGE

Shivering, Frenchy tries to ignore the men standing over him, asking him if he's all right.

He finds it hard to get a grip on the idea that a man can walk into a police station and start shooting. Not just any man, a man Frenchy had known when he was a kid. A man that must have been gunning for him.

In that single instant of recognition, in the initial flash of the 9mm's muzzle, Frenchy knew who the man was. Frenchy thought the man was dead.

An EMT places a small blanket over his shoulders. He looks up and thanks him, mouthing the words without sound. The name of the shooter slips him, but he thought he was dead. Him and the shooter's cousin, Smokey.

Frenchy looks down at the body of his possession arrest, Cortez. He can't decide why the man is lying there on the floor. The man was a civilian. Then Frenchy remembers he had picked him up on Essex Street, stumbling and harassing women on the street. Frenchy had found a small baggy of white powder. Frenchy figured heroin. The man was stoned. Now he was dead. Eventually it was bound to happen, Frenchy thinks. Everyone in Shawmut dies sooner than later.

The minute he saw the shooter and saw the muzzle flash his secret history came back. The flash, like a song in your head that you always hear and can't get out. The warm splash and ferric smell of blood like smelling freshly mown grass and thinking of a summer long past. Or, the ocean rolling in on an east wind unencumbered by the stench of jet fuel that always reminded Frenchy of a childhood spent on Revere Beach. The smell of burning and more flashes, one right after another brought the day back to Frenchy.

No one in Shawmut easily forgets that day. The investigators concluded the fire was not arson. Frenchy remembers the glee he felt as he and the shooter, Lefty – that was his name, Lefty – and the shooter's cousin, Smokey, lit each bale of old clothing.

Watch this Frenchy said to the other two boys, Smokey and his cousin Lefty. He pulled a match, lit it and stuck it in the matchbook and nestled it in a bale of rags. He remembers watching the city burn from Lefty's grandparents' apartment. That night the fire turned the city into a movie, scarred red and orange, glowing, all the blue smoked out of the sky and the ground and his eyes. Frenchy remembered Lefty saying he bet the fire could be seen from space, from the moon. If the astronauts could always see the fires of Bedouins in the Sahara, then they could see a city burning in North America.

But that secret history made Frenchy's stomach twist. He regretted lighting the fire, felt guilty about it, but never confessed the sin, never sought absolution. He had tried to smother the guilt with whoring and boozing in Montreal after high school. Then he tried to tar it over with good police work back in Shawmut.

Shawmut was the real problem. He should never have come back to Shawmut. He hates the city. He hates the narrow streets lined with sagging triple-deckers and covered with broken glass that sparkle in the dim streetlights like useless, dizzy gems. The bridge suffocates him. The politics, the infighting, the lack of a raise for years threaten to send him screaming over the side of the bridge. The rats in the basement of the station, the asbestos that dusts his locker and coats his uniform every time he changes, pushes him to edge. He has never bothered learning Spanish and feels himself at a loss in the streets confronting teenage gangbangers, distraught mothers and undocumented laborers. He can't comprehend that the corner stores once run by Hy, or Saul, have become bodegas, Spanish markets that sell rice and beans in five pound bags and advertise goat meat. Frenchy doesn't care who runs the stores. He doesn't feel welcome in them. The uniform has something to do with it, but it's the vibe. It's no longer his city. When he returned from Montreal he sensed things had changed, but he didn't believe it. When he joined the police department, he still wasn't sure. In the streets of the two square mile city he found out quickly how things had changed. He realizes he feels ambivalent about the changes, doesn't give a rat's ass whether the city burns once more or becomes a new San Juan or Santo Domingo.

Frenchy watches the EMTs and firefighters carry the dead out. No one bothers him.

He felt dead. When you die, he had heard, your life flashes before your eyes. Now, Frenchy saw his life cascading like a film running through a bad projector, jumpy, grainy and burning holes when the spools stuck. Pinpointing the moment that lead to him sitting on the police station floor was not easy. He jumps back to Montreal, running on Rue Sainte-Catherine. He wishes he had never left. He had met a French girl, a friend of a cousin and should have stayed up there. But everything, even in Montreal pointed back to Shawmut.

This was the end he told himself. This was it. No more. He would quit the department and take a pension for disability. He could say the shooting had destroyed him mentally. He could no longer work in Shawmut. There were too many ghosts crowding the sidewalks.

He told himself he would move to Maine. Buy a cabin deep in the north woods. His nearest neighbors would be moose and deer and birds. It would always be cold and he could cut down trees for firewood and hunt for deer in the fall and grow his food during the summer.

No more pregnant teenagers on crack.
No more fighting politicians.
No more asbestos on his clothes.
No more nights in the Broadway Pub, at the end of the bar, alone.
No more fear.
No more Shawmut under the bridge.

Frenchy stands up and walks out of the police station. At the door the Chief stops him.

That was a brave thing you done, Frenchy. A damn brave thing. I was just saying to Mulcahy, I said, that Frenchy done a damn brave thing. Didn't I Mulcahy? Didn't I say that? the Chief turns to Mulcahy grinning. You sure did Chief. Brave. But poor Garvin. He only had eight months before his retirement.

Eight months. Imagine that, Frenchy. Poor bastard. It's unbelievable how this atrocity coulda happen. As I was saying to Mulcahy, we gotta get security under control around here. Didn't I say that Mulcahy?

Fuck it, none of it matters, Chief, Frenchy says.

You must be upset. Mulcahy, Frenchy must be upset. Can't blame him, I suppose. Poor Garvin. Imagine how upset his wife is gonna be.

Fuck Garvin. His wife hated him. He was an asshole, Frenchy hands his gun and badge to the Chief. I knew the shooter, Chief. I knew that fucking guy. We hung out as kids. He was Smokey's cousin, name a Lefty. Thought he was dead. But no, fuck, here he is shooting at me, trying to fucking kill me. I got no explanation why. But it had to be me. We hung out as kids. We started the fucking fire in '73. Did you know that, Chief? Did you know that, Mulcahy? Where was you that day?

Frenchy pushes past them and walks down the steps. He walks past the television vans setting up their remote broadcasts. He walks past the crowds gathered in a semicircle in front of the crumbling hundred year-old building. Frenchy walks across the street and heads to the bridge.

He heads to the bridge because he knows it leads north to Route One and Maine. But he also knows the bridge leads south to Florida, knows the southbound upper deck is almost two hundred feet above the Mystic River. They say when you hit the water from that height it's like hitting a cement floor. Frenchy remembers his father coming home from work at the fire station and saying we pulled another one out of the water. Another jumper. Put the car in park on the bridge and run to the side and over the railing. Maybe they think before jumping, maybe they just do it, no thought, that way they won't chicken out. Maybe some of them stop the car, walk to the edge of the bridge and hesitate. All that no longer matters to Frenchy. He could go either way, north or south or down.

WAR IN THE TIME OF LOVE

Galen first met Frenchy in a photography workshop at an artist's retreat in Skowhegan. In the darkroom, his tattoos looked like fire under water, seething boiling black ink in the red light. But the eagles on the back of his neck, like yin and yang totems, she wanted to devour, to lick their secret animal spirits, to find out what protected him. She saved the eagles for last. First, she swallowed the shark's teeth tattooed around his neck.

Galen told him she's always waiting for a new beginning, a new somewhere that isn't here. Frenchy can see it in her eyes, the way the tears always stay behind those imperfectly hazel irises and never come out.

Galen says she's never fucked in the shower and she's fucked everywhere. When she comes, her mouth taste like a glacier. The whole bathroom feels rubbery and tastes soapy and she smells like the cleanest person in the world.

Galen says she used to cut herself. Frenchy says the first time he got hit by a car he wasn't sure if he didn't will it to happen. That he might have avoided all that pain, but didn't want to. Like with my tattoos I don't want to avoid the pain, he says. It's like cutting myself because I want to feel something.

Galen understands this when she's licking his tattoos and tasting the pain that still surfaces. Every cut, every tattoo and piercing is a new release, a new revolution of pain.

At a Vietnamese restaurant, on their second date, Galen kept wiping lipstick off her tea cup. Frenchy liked the way her finger lingered over the russet smudge. He wanted to taste the tea cup and her finger and her mouth.

They faded after each caress like misspent meteorites, flashing across the sky in the rubbery embrace of gravity. They touched moons and tasted stars, seas, salts, salvation. They crackled with light, with love and desire, with mania and depression, with dread at the edge of the universe.

You need a goal in life, Galen said. Imagine a mountain, its base reaching deep in the earth. The ocean is a cryptic wonder, she said. Your eyes are bluer when you stand in the light.

In your mind, touch that soft spot below my neck, between my collar bone, Galen said. Now the furrow behind my ear lobe. Next touch the web between my index finger and thumb and feel the piece of glass still embedded beneath my skin from when I fell as a young girl.

Galen's hazel eyes and her messy rust-colored hair and green sweatshirt made Frenchy think she was one of her own collages. A work-in-progress, a series of sketches on beauty. Frenchy leaned over and kissed her.

They watched snow come down at first in fitful opaque flakes. Then the storm grew until it looked like the sky was filled with snow falling furiously and obliquely. The next night, Frenchy couldn't sleep. He listened to Galen's breathing and thought it sounded like the snow that appeared like ghost kisses on the window, sticking and then melting.

Under the stars, near the ocean, in the forest, Frenchy felt the world around him slip by. It dissolved into shadows that lingered just out of focus. The world no longer became necessary. Frenchy had Galen. The stars pregnant with light, the ocean and the forest dancing around each other at the edge of the continent. Everything else existed in a land de-populated by the living where Frenchy had once existed for so long. It was the only reality he needed. Every wicked thing in Frenchy's past had disappeared. Even smell no longer triggered bad memories. When Frenchy smelled the ocean, he thought of Galen. When he smelled the woods, he thought of Galen. When Frenchy smelled newly mown hay, he thought only of Galen. When Frenchy smelled fire, wood burning, he thought only of Galen.

In the morning after the storm, before they went out to shovel Galen made coffee while Frenchy mixed an apple in his oatmeal.

Frenchy stopped and kissed the back of Galen's neck. He picked up her left hand and kissed the web between her index finger and thumb and felt the glass still embedded under her skin from when she fell as a young girl.

Coffee's gonna get cold, Galen wanted to say, but her words got lost in an airless maze when Frenchy pulled down her t-shirt and kissed that furrow between the ends of her collar bone under her neck. She felt him grow hard, but she wanted this to be her time. *You're oatmeal's going to get cold*, she said, her words suddenly unmazed.

Frenchy looked up and laughed. He lifted her shirt and pulled her leggings and underwear down a little off her hips and knelt in front of her, tracing the letters of the tattoo between her hip bones with his tongue.

I am Not Afraid Of Storms

Galen felt as if Frenchy had taken all the air out of her. She pushed her leggings and underwear down further. Frenchy pulled them the rest of the way to the floor. She leaned back against the table.

A flush crept up from Galen's chest to her neck. She must have moaned, but even that sound was lost in the airless maze.

The phone rang and Frenchy stopped. Galen held his head down. The phone stopped ringing.

In high school, Frenchy dated the girl who tattooed three lines on her left forearm with a threaded needle and ink. He drove her and her friends around even though his car had lost its power steering and three point turns felt like rounding the Horn.

She and her friends talked about their periods and masturbating in the shower and told him to pretend he was a girl and knew all about vaginas and cramps, but to shut up. So he listened and learned and understood this was a world he could only visit.

He navigated another three-point turn.

They all felt sorry for him, so the girl with the three tattooed lines grabbed his crotch. He's got a boner, she said. They all laughed.

But he still had to navigate the three point turns while they talked and laughed about other boys. How this one kissed like he would kiss his grandmother. And that one left her face slobbered over. How another would wash his hands after he fingered her.

He cheated on the girl with the tattooed lines. He didn't understand why. He liked the girl with the tattooed lines. He liked all her friends. But it was the girl with sepia-colored hair that looked at him in a way the girl with the tattooed lines did not.

One day, after class, he saw the girl with the sepia-colored hair walking alone. I want to show you something, she said. She unzipped her shorts. He was surprised she wore no underwear. Her hair felt soft and she was already wet.

When the engine seized and he had the car towed to the scrap yard, he stopped seeing the girl with the three tattooed lines and her friends. Without a car, he was back to being a boy. They said hi in the hall but the girl with the sepia-colored hair only smiled and kept walking.

Frenchy wasn't sure why he told Galen that. It was segue that made no sense. They had driven back down to Boston and Galen suggested they go to the Fogg Museum. They stood in front of the Van Gogh self-portrait, the one he dedicated to Paul Gaughin, the one the Nazis stole, the one with the veronese green background.

Galen said ok, so what. Look at that green. If I could paint green like that, I would feel complete, Don't you feel complete with me, Frenchy said. Don't you feel complete when I make you cum?Don't you feel complete when we're walking the woods, or walking on the beach? Galen looked at him and smiled.

Back home in Maine, Galen walks down the road as it runs along the coast. She can hear the waves and the wind as struggles through the firs on the landward side of the road. Galen briefly thinks it's too stormy to walk, but she walks anyway feeling a sadness descend upon her much as the cynical wind swallows her face. The sky over the coast changes from one minute to the next. always settling into a kind of dusty blue scratched with a dingy white before rearing up in an ugly black. Colors, Galen believes, are never as vibrant or alive as they appear during a thunderstorm. Color sucks in the energy of the storm. Color becomes a fourth category: plant animal, mineral, color.

When Galen gets home, she takes off her shoes and leaves them in the middle of the front hall; she takes off her wet clothes and leaves them in a pile in the kitchen. Naked and shovering, she puts in a CD she made for these sad days. She lies down on the couch.

First, there is Wagner's the Overture to *Tristan and Isolde*. She is crying by its end, knowing the story, knowing the tragedy of the lovers. Next Albinoni's *Adgio in G*. Then Barber's *Adagio for Strings*. Rachmaninov's

Isle of the Dead finishes the disc. Galen is still crying, picturing herself transported on a longship to that fabled land, where the ghosts exist like so many black pages in *Tristram Shandy* as voids of light of color.

When Frenchy dream about death, he sees himself walking in that similar charcoal void. He looks from right to left, not sure what may be lurking just inside the shadows that he passes. Frenchy dreams about death often, his own death. The images of his death always flickered, shot through with electrical turbulence. At times the dreams blurred, he saw nebulous actions, people speaking a language only he comprehended. Still, he understood the logic behind the images, the hyper motion, their links to each other and the wavelike flow that images adhere to in their progression from light to dark, from day to night, from life to death.

When Frenchy dreams of deaths other than his own, he sees funeral pyres by the Ganges, a man sitting up with the help of his wife so that he may face Mecca, a cleansing fire engulfing a longboat adrift on the ocean. But in all the dreams, the ending never changes, it remains a charcoal circle of ash first clustered then scattered by waves on the ocean.

Each day that Frenchy remodeled Galen's house, she would make him lunch. They left food in her bed, on the kitchen table, the countertops, the living room couch, the coffee table, the rug in the den, the shower and on the back porch. At the end of the day, he was famished and the taste and smell of her, mixed with sawdust, felt like stars in his mouth.

Galen wanted his life and energy. She wanted his energy to rid her of the dread that often overtook her when she couldn't paint. When they hugged, she said electricity arced between them like a Tesla experiment. When they fucked, the whole universe exploded, creating black holes and new stars alike. She said they were more than soul mates, they were twin flames. Both fire signs, creating conflagrations that burned out of control.

There were no fights, no screaming matches, just two misspent comets whose trajectories had split and pushed each other further out in the solar system. When they finally broke up, Galen's mother told her they'd end up back together in their eighties and die in each other's arms.

By then the war would be over and there would be nothing left but love.

This is how they left the 21st Century.

NOTES

Parts of The Hagiography of Sonny Drinkwater
appeared as verse in *Lily Poetry Review.*
Parts of The Tattoos of June and Otzi appeared in
Secret Histories.
Parts of Smokey of the Migraines appeared as verse in
Nixes Mate Review.
Parts of War in the Time of Love appeared in *Secret
Histories.*
The Beretta Sales Sheet excerpts can be found at:
beretta.com/en-us/product/92fs-inox-FA0173

ABOUT THE AUTHOR

Len Quimby lives in a cabin over looking a kettle pond in eastern Penobscot County, Maine. He has worked construction, fishing, and most recently blueberry cultivation. *War in the Time of Love* is his first novella.

PRIMAL PUBLISHING
PO Box 1179 · Allston, MA 02134
primal.pub

9 781971 785004